Wordplay

A TOON BOOK BY

ivan brunetti

For Laura

Editorial Director: FRANÇOISE MOULY

Book Design: IVAN BRUNETTI & FRANÇOISE MOULY

IVAN BRUNETTI'S artwork was done in India ink and colored digitally.

A TOON Book™ © 2017 Ivan Brunetti & TOON Books, an imprint of Raw Junior, LLC, 27 Greene Street, New York, NY 10013. No part of this book may be used or reproduced in any manner whatsoever without written permission except in the case of brief quotations embodied in critical articles and reviews. TOON Graphics™, TOON Books®, LITTLE LIT® and TOON Into Reading!™ are trademarks of RAW Junior, LLC. All rights reserved. All our books are Smyth Sewn (the highest library-quality binding available) and printed with soy-based inks on acid-free, woodfree paper harvested from responsible sources. Printed in China by C&C Offset Printing Co., Ltd. Distributed to the trade by Consortium Book Sales; orders (800) 283-3572; orderentry@perseusbooks.com; www.cbsd.com. Library of Congress Cataloging-in-Publication Data: Brunetti, Ivan, author, illustrator. Wordplay : a TOON book / by Ivan Brunetti. New York, NY : TOON Books, [2017] Summary: In this hilarious introduction to compound words by a famed cartoonist, a young student named Annemarie learns how to have fun with language.– Provided by publisher. Identifiers: LCCN 2016036358 | ISBN 9781943145171 (hardcover : alk. paper) Subjects: LCSH: Graphic novels. | CYAC: Graphic novels. | English language– Compound words–Fiction. Classification: LCC PZ7.7.B813 Wo 2017 | DDC 741.5/973--dc23 LC record available at https://lccn.loc.gov/2016036358
ISBN: 978-1-943145-17-1 (hardcover)
17 18 19 20 21 22 C&C 10 9 8 7 6 5 4 3 2 1

ABOUT THE AUTHOR

IVAN BRUNETTI began to learn English when he was eight years old, after his family moved from Italy to America. He says, "I usually see letters and words as shapes, and I like twisting them, taking them apart, flipping them upside down, mixing, blending, and rearranging them."

Ivan has published many acclaimed books for adults, including *Cartooning: Philosophy and Practice*, but this is his first book for children. He wrote *Wordplay* to share his love of language with young readers: "English helped me relax and be myself and transformed me into the person I am today."

pal rowdy law day pad rap
paw royal owl
word draw drop
row world way low
plow yard play
ado raw
lady ploy ray
drawl wary pow

I also like to play with the *LETTERS* in the words.

HOW TO READ COMICS WITH KIDS

Kids love comics! They are naturally drawn to the pictures, which makes them want to read the words. Comics beg for repeated readings and are a great way to introduce complex stories with a rich vocabulary. But since comics have their own grammar, here are a few tips for reading them with kids:

GUIDE YOUNG READERS: Use your finger to show your place in the text, but keep it at the bottom of the character speaking so it doesn't hide the very important facial expressions.

HAM IT UP! Think of the comic book story as a play, and don't hesitate to read with expression and intonation. Assign parts or get kids to supply the sound effects, a great way to reinforce phonics skills.

LET THEM GUESS: Comics provide lots of context for the words, so emerging readers can make informed guesses. Like jigsaw puzzles, comics ask readers to make connections, so check children's understanding by asking "What's this character thinking?" (but don't be surprised if a kid finds some of the comics' subtle details faster than you).

TALK ABOUT THE PICTURES: Point out how the artist paces the story with pauses (silent panels) or speeded-up action (a burst of short panels). Discuss how the size and shape of the panels convey meaning.

ABOVE ALL, ENJOY! There is of course never one right way to read, so go for the shared pleasure. Once children make the story happen in their imagination, they have discovered the thrill of reading, and you won't be able to stop them. At that point, just go get them more books, and more comics.

www.TOON-BOOKS.com

SEE OUR FREE ONLINE CARTOON MAKERS, LESSON PLANS, AND MUCH MORE